This book belongs to:

_____

For my grandchildren
Zoe, Stephen, Anna,
Jamie, Jude and Micah,
and those yet to be born. . .

— N. L.

To my lovely
*wife **Anna***
who is so full
of good things.

— B. H.

Copyright © 2007 by Neal Lozano

MAPLE CORNERS PRESS *is an imprint of*
THE ATTIC STUDIO Publishing House • P.O. Box 75 • Clinton Corners, NY 12514
Phone: 845-266-8100 • *Fax:* 845-266-5515 • *E-mail:* AtticStudioPress@aol.com

PRINTED IN THE UNITED STATES OF AMERICA   5 4 3 2 1 FIRST EDITION

Library of Congress Cataloging-in-Publication Data

Lozano, Neal, 1949-
    Can God see me in the dark? / by Neal Lozano ; with pictures by Ben Hatke. —1st ed.
      p. cm.
    Summary: When Anna goes to sleep overnight at her grandparents' house for the very first time, she is afraid of the dark, but her grandfather explains that Jesus is with her even when she cannot see, which makes her feel better.
    ISBN 978-1-883551-45-2 (alk. paper)
      [1. Sleepovers—Fiction. 2. Fear of the dark—Fiction. 3. Grandparents—Fiction. 4. Christian life—Fiction.] I. Hatke, Ben, ill. II. Title.
          PZ7.L96765Can 2007
          [E]—dc22

                            2007010949

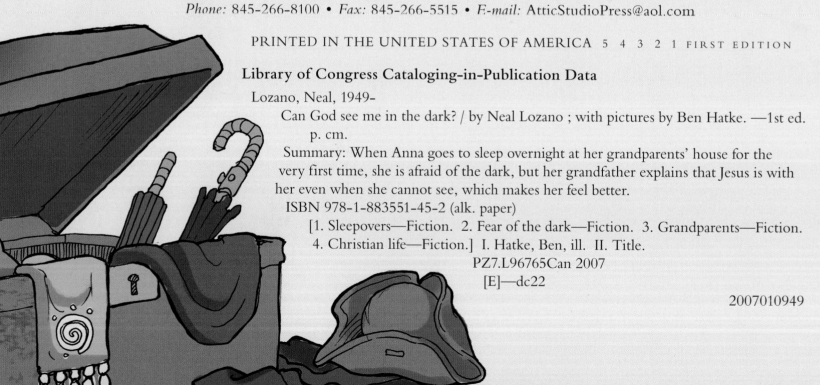

Can God see me in the Dark?

by Neal Lozano

with pictures by Ben Hatke

Maple
Corners
Press

Maple Corners Press

CLINTON CORNERS, NEW YORK

"Goppy, Goppy, Goppy!" Anna giggled.

Goppy was a happy name. Anna loved saying it three times fast as she danced and twirled around the bedroom. She felt just like a butterfly about to take flight.

This was a special night. Anna was sleeping over at Goppy and Gammy's house for the very first time— all by her very grown-up self!

Anna loved the big, old house with all its nooks and crannies that were perfect for hide 'n seek. And she loved the big bedroom with its soft-as-a-cloud bed. And she especially loved the big wooden armoire, packed with the toys and treasures of other boys and girls who had laughed and played in this room.

But most of all, Anna loved Goppy
and Gammy, and the big, big love she
felt whenever she was with them.

Anna took one last twirl as Goppy
came in to kiss her goodnight.

"Hop into bed, Anna Banana," he said.

And in one flying leap, Anna was up to her ears in pillows and covers.

Anna's grandfather smoothed the blankets, being careful not to disturb Simon the Snowbear, who looked drowsy and ready for sleep. Then they all closed their eyes, and Goppy prayed a special blessing just for Anna.

"Lord Jesus, thank You for Anna
and for the wonderful plans
You have for her life.
Thank You that I can see
Your joy and love in Anna.
Please watch over her as she sleeps."

Her grandfather kissed Anna's forehead tenderly. Then he turned out the light and left the room.

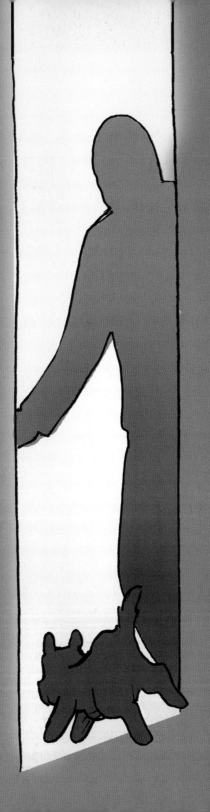

Anna was alone. And somehow
the big room wasn't as friendly in
the dark. Suddenly Anna wanted
her own room and her own bed—
and most of all she wanted her
Goppy to come back.

So Anna popped out of bed
and swung open the door.

"Goppy," she called,
"can God see me in the dark?"

Anna's grandfather picked her up and carried her back to bed. He took her tiny hands in his. "Anna," he said, "close your eyes really tight. Now what do you see?"

"I see dark," said Anna.

"Good!" said Goppy. "Now tell me, what am I doing?"

"You're . . . you're . . ." Anna thought hard until she found the answer. "You're looking at me, Goppy!"

"Right you are! And what else am I doing?"

Reaching up, Anna touched her grandfather's bushy eyebrows and scratchy whiskers. The expression she felt on his face made her laugh.

"You're smiling," she giggled. "Smiling at me!"

"Right again, Anna Banana. And what comes next?"

By now Anna was good at this game. "You're gonna kiss me right here, Goppy. And you're going to say 'Anna Banana, I love you!'"

And that's exactly what Goppy did.

"When you know somebody, you don't need eyes to see them," he said as he smoothed Anna's tousled brown hair. "You can see them with the eyes of your heart."

"That's how we see Jesus — with our hearts."

"When Jesus died," Goppy told Anna, "His friends were sad because they couldn't see Him or touch Him. But when He rose from the dead, they were happy again. His friend Thomas, who didn't believe Jesus was alive, was able to touch Him and see Him like before. They even had dinner together."

"Then Jesus left again, only this time He went up to heaven to be with His Father. His friends were both happy and sad at the same time. Happy that Jesus promised to always be with them, and happy that He promised to send them a special gift. But sad because they missed Jesus. Not being able to see or touch Him made them feel very alone.

So they waited and waited ... and prayed and prayed."

"Then, on a special day of the year called Pentecost, the gift arrived. It was the Holy Spirit! The Holy Spirit came like the wind, and when He came into their hearts, He opened the eyes of their hearts.

Jesus' friends were so happy they laughed and laughed and laughed — because now they could see Jesus again! And they left that place telling everyone about Jesus."

"That's how we know and see Jesus, Anna Banana —
with the eyes of our hearts.

And that's how Jesus sees you, too.
Jesus knows you. And He loves you.
So He always sees you, even when it's dark."

Just the thought of it made Anna feel happy inside. Closing her eyes, she waited for Goppy to go on.

"Anna," he said gently, "think about Jesus sitting right here beside you. Can you picture Him here?"

Anna nodded, shutting her eyes even tighter.

"What is He doing?" her grandfather whispered.

"He's looking at me!" said Anna.

"What else is He doing?" asked Goppy.

"He's smiling at me!" she said.

"And what is He going to do next?"

Anna's eyes popped open.

"He's going to kiss me right here. And say 'Anna Banana,
I love you. And I'll be watching over you all night.'"

Goppy reached over to turn out the light.

"Good night, sweet Anna!" he said to the little girl
in the soft-as-a-cloud bed.

"Good night, Goppy," said Anna.

And it was a good night . . . a very blessed night indeed.

A Note to Parents, Grandparents & Caregivers

God has given your children a great gift. That gift is you. You have been entrusted with His love for them, as well as keys to His Kingdom. You, like no one else, can "enlighten the eyes of their hearts" (Eph. 1:18).

Long before the Holy Spirit opened the eyes of the hearts of the disciples, Jesus spent time with them. He loved them, always pointing beyond Himself to His Father and the Kingdom of Heaven. Jesus said, "Anyone who has seen me has seen the Father" (John 14:9). And, "If you knew me, you would know my Father also" (John 8:19).

This is where it starts: Inviting your children to see and know you. Then helping them to use their imaginations so that they can see what you see.

———————————————

For additional copies of **Can God See Me in the Dark?** please visit your local bookstore, or call 610-952-4871, or visit our special website: **www.willyoublessme.com**

One day, just like the disciples, your children will need to see Jesus — and by God's grace, they will. They will see for themselves what you helped them understand in the tender moments when you patiently responded to the needs of their hearts, expressed in questions like: "Can God see me in the dark?"

If you are interested in learning more about how to bless your child, please visit: www.willyoublessme.com

Blessings,

Neal Joyner